LUCKY ME

LUCKY ME
BY
DENYS CAZET

~ BRADBURY · PRESS ~
~ SCARSDALE, N.Y

LEGAL NOTICE

Text and Illustrations copyright © 1983 by Denys Cazet. All rights reserved. No part of this book may be reproduced in any form or by any means, with the exception of brief quotations in a review, without permission in writing from the publisher. Manufactured in the United States of America.   2

The text of this book is set in 16 pt Goudy Old Style.

Library of Congress Cataloging in Publication Data

Cazet, Denys. Lucky me.

Summary: Beginning with the lucky chicken who finds a donut, each subsequent animal in this cumulative tale feels he has found a tasty morsel until an army of ants spoils the "picnic" for them all.

[1. Animals — Fiction]   I. Title.

PZ7. C2985Lu   [E]   AACR2

ISBN 0-02-717870-6

A PUBLIC ANNOUNCEMENT

✦ ✦ ✦

THIS BOOK IS FOR ✦ALEX✦

Lucky Me ♥ Denys

STAGE DO

501 THEATER

TICKETS NOW FOR THE

DREAM FLUF

BAKERY

PRICES SUBJECT TO CHANGE

Get 'em while they're HOT!!

TODAY ONLY free while they last...

FREE DONUT

HOW ABOUT SOME LEMONADE WITH YOUR FREE DONUT 5¢

One spring morning a lovely chicken named Marie brought a pie to her friends, the Goslings. And the Goslings gave Marie a present for her family.

On her way home, Marie passed a bakery.

The baker gave Marie two free donuts.

"Lucky me!" said Marie.

Marie put the donuts into her bag with the present and crossed the street.

As she stepped onto the sidewalk, her heart went thump!

Marie saw a fox whose name was Flashy Jake. He was an uptown fox as slick as he was hungry. He licked his hungry lips as Marie walked by.

"Lucky me!" he said.

"Cluck!" said Marie.

GREEN AL'S

HAIR CUTS WHILE YOU WAIT

Just as Flashy Jake caught up with Marie he saw a dog whose name was Truenose.

Truenose was a down and out dog with a nose for a truly tasty fox with a side order of chicken.

"Lucky me!" he said.

"Oh, oh!" said the fox.

"Cluck!" said Marie.

WAREHOUSE ENTRANCE

THIS SIDE UP

HANDLE WITH CARE

NO PARKING

Just as Truenose caught up with Flashy Jake and Marie, he saw a mountain lion whose name was Sharpclaws.

Sharpclaws' stomach growled a hollow growl as he stretched his long and sharp claws.

"Lucky me!" he said.

"Yipes!" said the dog.

"Oh, oh!" said the fox.

"Cluck!" said Marie.

Just as Sharpclaws caught up with True-nose, Flashy Jake and Marie, a sourpuss of a bear came running around the corner.

His name was Munchandcrunch. A long winter's nap had made him very, very hungry.

"Yummy!" said the bear as he followed them into a park. "Just what I've been looking for . . . a four course dinner.

"Lucky me!" he said.

"Me-ow!" said the mountain lion.

"Yipes!" said the dog.

"Oh, oh!" said the fox.

"Cluck!" said Marie.

DR. BONALD HALL
BOTANICAL GARDENS
CITY
PARK
～MAYOR F. RODRIQUEZ～
P. CONDON · CONTRACTOR · 1957

"STOP! And sit down!" shouted the bear. The others all sat down on a see-saw.

"Yum, yum, yummy," said the bear, "four tasties for brunch! Where will I start?"

"Start with the dog," said the mountain lion.

"Start with the fox," said the dog.

"Start with the chicken," said the fox.

Marie looked around. There was no one behind her except two little rabbits sitting in a sand box.

"Cluck!" said Marie.

"Hummph!" Munchandcrunch snorted. "I think I'll just sit down and study the menu."

But, as sometimes happens, the biggest did not pay attention to the smallest.

Munchandcrunch sat on the opposite end of the see-saw — but on a family of red ants!

Their names were

If you sit on us we will bite you where you sit.

And, true to their names . . .

. . . that's what they did!
"YEEEOUCH!" screeched the bear.
He flew up into the air
and everyone else came down
with a thump on the ground.

When the bear came crashing down
the others flipped up into the sky.

Marie landed in the sand box.

The dog and the mountain lion fell on top of the bear.

The fox bounced over the see-saw and ran toward the gate. "This fox is too smart to be anyone's lunch!" he shouted. "Run legs, run!"

"Bye-bye, Dullpaws!" Truenose shouted. "I'm heading home on the fastest feet in town!"

"Catch you later, Phewnose!" the mountain lion growled. "This cat isn't going to be in the middle of any fat bear's sandwich!" Sharpclaws jumped over the park wall.

Munchandcrunch shouted and stomped and slapped his bottom all the way out of the park.

D. M. MAURER
PLAYGROUND
CITY
PARK

Soon, it was quiet. Everyone was gone.
Except the two little rabbits.
　And the ants.
　And Marie.
　Marie took one donut out of her bag
and gave it to the two little rabbits.
　"Lucky us!" said the rabbits.
　She took the other donut out
and gave it to the ants.
　"Lucky us!" said the ants.
　"Lucky me!" said Marie.

"Home at last," smiled Marie.
"Lucky, lucky me."

FOX ARRESTED IN 5TH ST HENHOUSE

TWEET TIMES

PRESIDENT NAMES NEW PECKING ORDER

CACKLE COMICS

"Look at what the Goslings sent us," Marie said to her family. "DONUTS! What a nice surprise!"

"Aren't we lucky!" said Pop Rooster.

"Cluck!" said Marie.